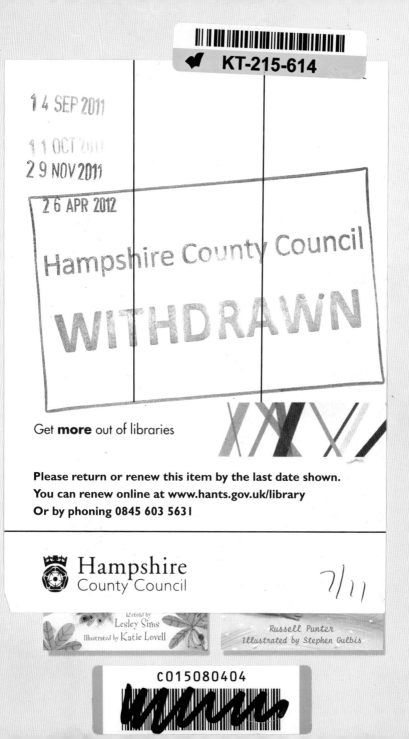

Get **more** out of libraries

Please return or renew this item by the last date shown.
You can renew online at www.hants.gov.uk/library
Or by phoning 0845 603 5631

Hampshire
County Council

7/11

Retold by
Lesley Sims
Illustrated by Katie Lovell

Russell Punter
Illustrated by Stephen Gulbis

How Zebras Got Stripes
Their

A tale from Africa

Retold by Lesley Sims

Illustrated by Laure Fournier

Reading consultant: Alison Kelly
Roehampton University

This story is about

a greedy
baboon,

a pond,

a giraffe,

an elephant

and the
very first
zebra.

Long ago, there was a greedy baboon.

He lived by a pond.

He wanted the pond all
to himself.

Everyone was thirsty.

Baboon didn't care.

Giraffe crept to
the pond.

Baboon **roared**.
He waved his arms and
jumped up and down.

Giraffe fled.

Elephant went to
the pond.

Baboon **roared**. He jumped up and down and waved his arms.

Elephant fled.

Zebra walked up.

Baboon **roared**.
Zebra stamped his hoof.

"It's not your pond," he said. "You must share it."

"No!" said Baboon.
"Go away."

Baboon got lots of sticks.

He piled them by
the pond.

Then he lit a big fire.

Zebra wasn't scared.

He ran at Baboon.

He kicked out his legs.

Baboon flew into
the air.

So did the
sooty sticks
from the fire.

The sticks landed
on Zebra.

Baboon landed on
his bottom.

Ever since then, zebras
have had black stripes.

And baboons have had
red bottoms.

PUZZLES

Puzzle 1
Put the pictures in order.

A

B

C

D

E

F

Puzzle 2

A

B

C

Can you spot
the mistake in
each picture?

Puzzle 3
Choose the best sentence.

Puzzle 4

Can you find these things in the picture?

Elephant	Giraffe	pond
Zebra	Baboon	tail
bananas	trunk	

Answers to puzzles

Puzzle 1

E

D

F

C

A

B

Puzzle 2

A

B

C

Blue snake

Spots on Zebra

Different fruit

Puzzle 3

A — Giraffe has spots!

B — Baboon is greedy!

Puzzle 4

About the story

This story is based on an old folk tale from Namibia in Africa.

Designed by Nancy Leschnikoff
Additional design by Emily Bornoff
Series designer: Russell Punter

First published in 2009 by Usborne Publishing Ltd., Usborne House, 83-85 Saffron Hill, London EC1N 8RT, England. www.usborne.com
Copyright © 2009 Usborne Publishing Ltd.

USBORNE FIRST READING
Level Three

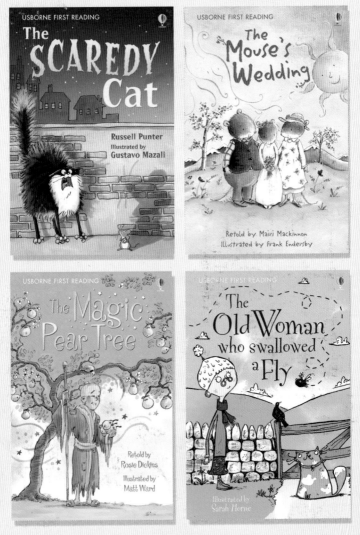

USBORNE FIRST READING

The SCAREDY Cat

Russell Punter
Illustrated by
Gustavo Mazali

USBORNE FIRST READING

The Mouse's Wedding

Retold by Mairi Mackinnon
Illustrated by Frank Endersby

USBORNE FIRST READING

The Magic Pear Tree

Retold by
Rosie Dickins
Illustrated by
Matt Ward

USBORNE FIRST READING

The Old Woman who swallowed a Fly

Illustrated by
Sarah Horne